Victoria

SHADOW CHASER

by
Stephen Cosgrove
Illustrated by
Wendy Edelson

MULTNOMAH

10209 SE Division Street, Portland, Oregon 97266

Library of Congress Cataloging-in Publication Data

Cosgrove, Stephen.
   Shadow chaser / written by Stephen Edward Cosgrove;
illustrated by Wendy Edelson.

   Summary: All the animals are alarmed because Gabriel
Groundhog, quivering in fear of shadows, refuses to come
out of his burrow on Groundhog Day to signal the end of
winter.

   [1. Woodchuck—Fiction. 2. Groundhog Day—Fiction.
3. Shadows—Fiction. 4. Fear—Fiction] I. Edelson, Wendy,
ill. II. Title
PZ7.C8117Sg 1988   [E]   88-1533

91 92 93 94 95 96 97 98 - 9 8 7 6 5 4 3 2

Dedicated to Pastor Michael Anderson
When I was afraid and in the dark
Michael lit a candle that
illuminated my path.

arther than far and to the very edge of the horizon was a path bordered with lacy fern, now painted with the crystal snows of winter. If you walked down that path following a blue jay's tracks in the snow, you would find the land called Barely There.

Barely There . . . a land filled with untouched magic, where the wind whispers about the giant pines and barren oaks and whips snow-flakes high into the sky, only to return in lazy circles to the forest floor and the land called Barely There.

Down one of the snow-covered paths
was a meadow in the woods. It was oh, so
quiet, muffled by a deep blanket of snow.
Ghostly birch and poplar trees gently
moaned and creaked in the winter winds.

The meadow seemed undisturbed,
save for a mound of snow-covered dirt that
marked the entrance to a tunnel, a twisty
tunnel that ran this way and that. Down the

tunnel, lit by sputtering candles stuck haphazardly in the wall, was an old heavy plank door.

Beyond the door was a living room. In the living room was a fireplace filled with golden glowing embers of a dying fire.

Near the fireplace was yet another door left open just a crack to let a bit of light spill down the hall.

At the end of the shadowed hall was a bedroom. In this room was a wooden, rickety bed made of oak with willow ties. Sleeping in the bed was a grizzled old groundhog called Gabriel. Now, as we all know, groundhogs go to sleep in the early fall before the snows to dream the winter away.

Gabriel had gone to bed a little earlier than the other groundhogs, not because he was tired and not because he needed his sleep. Silly Gabriel had gone to bed because he was afraid of imaginary creatures that he thought hid in the winter's shadows. He felt that the best place to hide from his fears was behind a dream.

So, sleep and dream he did. His snores snarled about the room like the noise of a bee gone mad. "Zzzz! Snarkle! Zzzz!" He smiled in his sleep and muttered and tossed as he dreamed delightful dreams of bumblebees and butterflies.

Gabriel would have slept forever. He would have slept through spring and summer and winter again had there not come a tapping, rap-a-tap-rapping on his door. He woke with a "Shnuff!" thinking he had dreamed the knocking, but there it was again.

He squinted his eyes as he looked about the room and yawned once or twice. He looked at a shadow in the corner . . . over there! He looked and looked and the more he looked the more he saw, or at least he thought he saw. His hands shook a bit as he struck a match and lit the blackened wick on a much-used candle of sticky pitch. The candle flickered in the dark and then burst into light, chasing all the shadows from the room.

Sure that now he was safe as could be, Gabriel slipped into an old tattered robe and some warm wooley slippers.

From the door there came another tapping, rap-a-tap-rapping.

"Harrumph!" he muttered as he shuffled down the hall. "I wonder who could be tapping and rapping at my door in the middle of the night, in the middle of my sleep, in the middle of my dreams?" He peered into the living room sure that the room would be filled with shadow creatures of scary delight, but there was nothing there, nothing at all.

Once again there came a tapping, rap-a-tap-rapping.

With his candle held high he nervously opened the squeaking creaking door. There in the tunnel stood a small bunny, bundled up against the winter's chill.

"What do you want?" shouted a relieved but angry Gabriel. "You woke me up in the middle of the night in the middle of my dreams. You nearly scared me out of my wits."

"Oh, I am so sorry," apologized the bundled bunny in a tiny little voice. "I didn't come to scare you, but I did come to wake you. For you see, today is Groundhog Day. On Groundhog Day you are supposed to come outside and look for your shadow. If you find it we'll sadly have another month of winter, but if you don't, spring is on its way. But you must come outside or winter will never go away."

Gabriel looked at the bunny as if it had gone crazy. "I'm not going to look for my

shadow. Don't you know that scary things hide in shadows?"

"You must be joking," said the bunny, hiding a smile behind his mitten. "Come, it's time for you to look for your shadow." With that the bunny reached out to take Gabriel's hand.

The crotchety old groundhog looked at the bunny's hand in disbelief. "The only thing I'm going to look for is my bed!" Then he rudely slammed the door in the bunny's face.

With the shadows of his mind lurking everywhere, Gabriel once again gazed about the room with the candle held high. Then, sure that all was safe, he sheltered the flickering flame in his furry hand and shuffled back down the hall. He set the candle on the table and scooted into the safety of his bed between the cold slippery sheets and the warm woolen blanket.

That silly groundhog pulled the patch-work quilt of eiderdown up to his nose and nervously peeked this way and that. Through chattering teeth he murmured as he struggled to fall back asleep,

Shadows in the corner,
underneath the bed,
keep the candle burning,
keep the fire fed!

Far above the shadowy rooms, in the meadow above, the winter winds began to rage. Clouds boiled across the sky and cold crystal snow fell faster and faster. Here and there, huddled in the meadow, were the creatures of the forest who had come to ask the groundhog when winter would be over.

"He is scared of his shadow, I tell you," said the bundled bunny. "He just won't come out!"

"That's silly. If he doesn't come out we'll have winter forever," the other creatures chorused. "You must go ask him again or we will freeze and there'll be no blossoms on the trees."

Reluctantly, the bundled bunny hopped down the hole and into the twisted tunnel.

Along the tunnel he hopped to the groundhog's heavy plank door. Rap-a-tap-rap. Nothing happened, so he tapped again, rap-a-tap-rap.

From within he could hear the frightened, gravelly voice of Gabriel, "Go away you shadows. Go away. Just let this poor old groundhog get some sleep!"

The little bunny giggled as he listened to the foolish cries. But winter would last forever if Gabriel wouldn't come outside, so the bunny patiently knocked some more on the worn wooden door, rap-a-tap-rap. Rap-a-tap-rap!

Soon all the forest creatures made their way down the tunnel and gathered near the heavy plank door.

"He's so frightened of shadows he has never seen that he won't even look at his own," said the bunny.

"Well, we must do something or winter will never go away," the others muttered as they stomped their fuzzy feet and slapped

their sides trying to get warm. The creatures paced about the tunnel as they thought and thought, wondering what to do.

"I know what we should do," said the bundled bunny. "If the groundhog won't come looking for his shadow, let's take his shadow to him." With that he opened the creaking plank door and walked inside with the other forest creatures timidly following behind.

They marched past the fireplace and down the long hall to Gabriel's bedroom. There they found him huddled, shaking in fear beneath his quilt with his sputtering candle still lit beside the bed.

"Oh no!" he moaned. "The shadow monsters have come to take me away. Oh no!"

All the forest creatures began to laugh and laugh at the silly groundhog as he raved on and on. The more they laughed the more he shook in fear of nothing at all. The more he shook the more they laughed, the more they laughed the more he shook. This could have gone on forever.

"Shh!" said the bundled bunny as he quieted his forest friends. When all the creatures were quiet the bunny softly spoke, "Gabriel, there is nothing here to fear. We beg you, please get out of bed and come with us to the meadow. If you don't come out and look for your shadow, winter won't know when it's over and we'll have no spring."

Gabriel stuck his nose above the quilt and in a small frightened voice said, "But I am afraid of shadows!"

"Oh, but shadows are silly, shadows are fun," laughed the bundled bunny as he picked up the candle and with his mittened hand made a funny shadow on the wall.

Gabriel watched and slowly began to chuckle at the funny, fluttering shadow. Soon all the animals of the forest were making shadow creatures on the wall. They made butterflies and flutterbys. They made dogs that howled at the moon. They made spiders and tigers and even a funny bunny that walked on the wall. But most of all they made that silly old groundhog laugh and laugh at his own fears. The room filled with laughter and light as the silhouettes danced around the room.

With the help of his newfound friends, Gabriel put on his tattered scarf and his plaid patch hat and together they marched up the tunnel to the meadow above.

All the forest creatures stood to the side, leaving Gabriel alone in the middle of the meadow. He turned round and round and looked and looked. Nowhere could he find his shadow, and winter magically blew away.

As a small flower broke through the crust of winter snow, spring burst warmly into the land of Barely There . . . Barely There, a gentle land where friendship conquered fear, and darkness gave way to laughter and light.

Other books
in this series

Derby Downs
Fiddler
Gossamer
Hannah & Hickory
Ira Wordworthy
Persimmony
T.J. Flopp